HOW to Babysit a Logan

a Logan

By Callie Metler-Smith

Illustrated by Cindy Vattathil

Dedication:

For Sarah St. Cyr - Thank you for loving and guiding my Logan.
and For Cindy - You are the Cat's Meow,
thank you for bringing Thunderbolt to life in your art. - Callie

For my three little kittens, Lela, Henry and Melody,
and my purr-fect husband, Vimal - I love you all. - Cindy

How to Babysit a Logan

Text Copyright © 2019 by Callie Metler-Smith

Artwork Copyright © 2019 by Cindy Vattathil

SUMMARY – Thunderbolt the Cat takes his position of babysitting Logan, his human, very seriously. Logan has autism so it is Thunderbolt's job to protect and provide support for Logan throughout his day. In this heartfelt true story, view the world of living with someone with autism through the eyes of their beloved Cat.

Clear Fork Publishing
P.O. Box 870 - 102 S. Swenson
Stamford, Texas 79553
(325)773-5550 - www.clearforkpublishing.com

Printed and Bound in the United States of America.

Hardcover ISBN - 978-1-950169-08-5

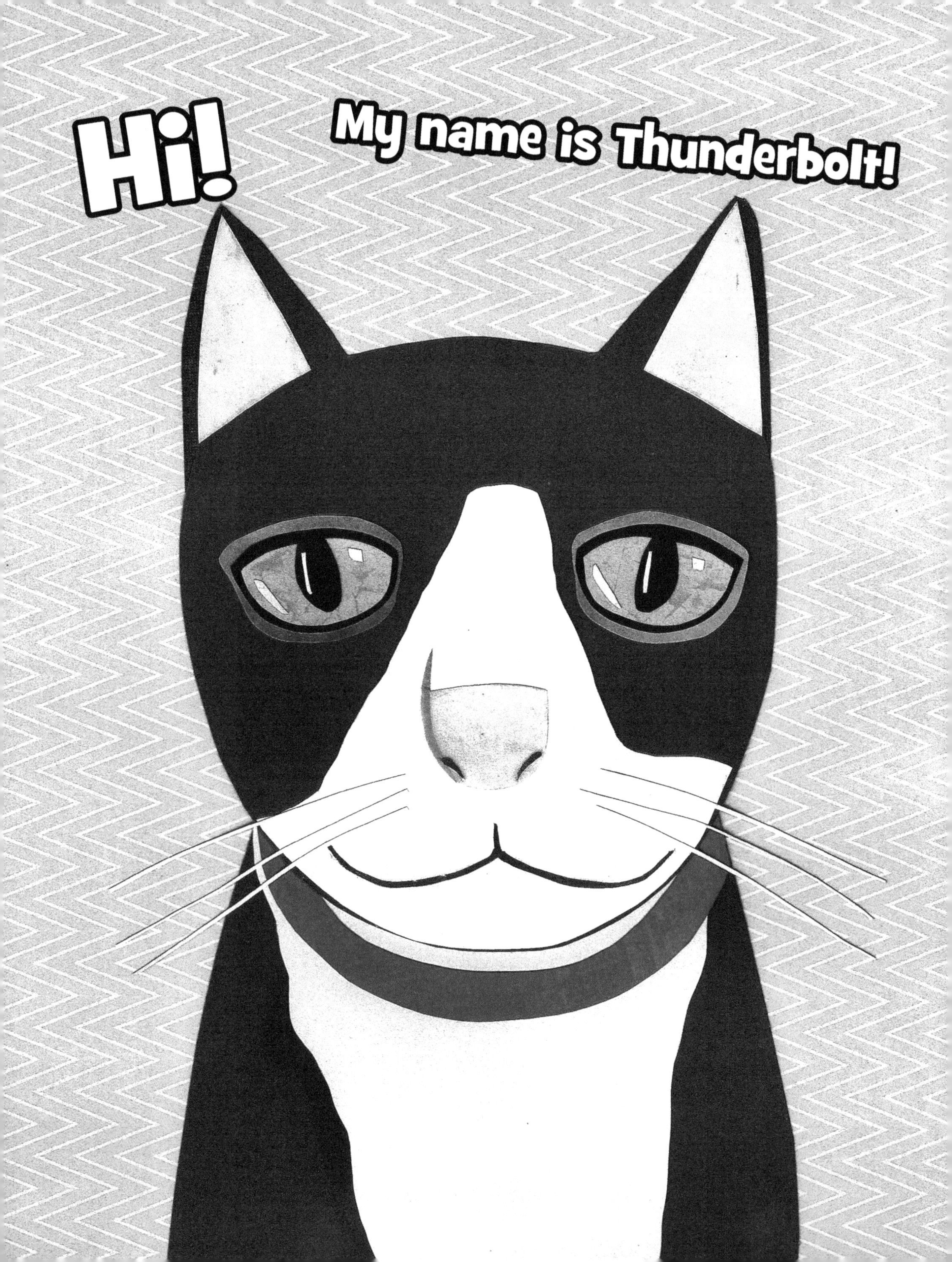
Hi!
My name is Thunderbolt!

My human, Logan, is asleep in bed. I watch over him because he has something called autism.

Autism is a super fancy word for the way Logan's brain works. The autism causes him to act differently than most humans.

Look!

It's time to snuggle with Logan before I wake him up for school!

I put my nose against his and nuzzle a little. I know I've done good when he says, "Good morning, Thunderbolt!"

Every morning, Logan takes a bath.

Logan hates water and so do I.
I make sure to perch on the counter so
Logan can see me and I don't get splashed.

After bathtime, Logan gets ready for school . . .

We inspect his jeans, they're just the right cotton.

Now for the shoes . . .
shoe strings . . . YUCK!

Next, I help him find a shirt without a collar.

I always make sure to rub against him, so he knows I am there. I meow, "Good choice, Logan. I like that shirt!"

While he's at school, I sleep on the couch.

I must conserve my energy for him.
I really miss him when he is gone.
I hover around the door so I will be the first thing
he sees when he gets home.

When Logan returns from school, he's usually tired from being around people all day.

He stretches on the couch and watches TV. I perch near him to show I missed him.

He always scratches me behind the ear. He missed me, too!

It's almost dinner time. I smell spaghetti cooking.

I make sure Logan's mom remembers to
keep the sauce off Logan's plate.
Logan doesn't like sauce. He only eats
the meatballs and noodles.

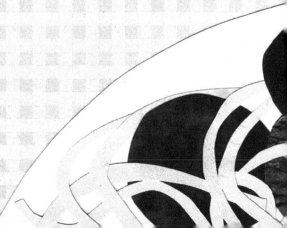

Yes! Logan drops one of the meatballs on the floor, on purpose.

I love Spaghetti Night! YUM!
I meow, "Thank you, Logan!"

After dinner, Logan heads to his room and is quiet. This is my favorite time of the day.

Logan prefers small spaces, so we sleep in a tent every night on his bed. I snuggle next to him as he folds his arms around me.

I love babysitting my Logan. It is my job to help him get through the day. I can't wait to see what tomorrow brings...

Author's Note

Thunderbolt came to our house in 2011 as a reward Logan got for keeping his room clean from the house fairy. They instantly became fast friends. I had read a study about how furry faced animals improved eye contact. It was obvious that Logan connected with Thunderbolt on a deeper level than anyone else. We soon noticed that Thunderbolt took his role of Logan's best friend very seriously. A few years ago Logan requested that I write a book about Thunderbolt, and I'm so pleased to share it with you now.

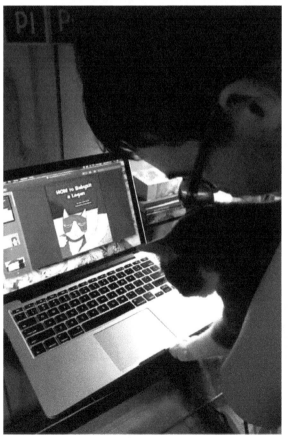

About the Author and Illustrator

Callie Metler-Smith is the owner of Clear Fork Media Group in Stamford, Texas. *How to Babysit a Logan* is her second children's book. When not working on her corner of the Square in Stamford, Texas, she is spending time with her husband, Philip and two sons, Logan and Ben and of course, Thunderbolt.

Cindy Vattathil is a self-taught collage artist from Houston, Texas. Like Thunderbolt, she loves spaghetti night and sleeping on the couch; however, despite a deep love of catnaps, she finds them rather elusive as a mother of three. *How to Babysit a Logan* is her first picture book.

9 781950 169085